Plowie

A STORY FROM THE PRAIRIE

PATRICIA KIRKPATRICK

Illustrated by

JOEY KIRKPATRICK

Harcourt Brace & Company
San Diego   New York   London

Library of Congress Cataloging-in-Publication Data
Kirkpatrick, Patricia.
Plowie: a story from the prairie/by Patricia Kirkpatrick; illustrations by
Joey Kirkpatrick. — 1st ed.
p.   cm.
Summary: A little girl finds a porcelain doll while helping her father with
the spring plowing; the doll, named Plowie, is handed down through
generations of family members.
ISBN 0-15-262802-9
[1. Dolls—Fiction. 2. Grandmothers—Fiction. 3. Farm life—Fiction.]
I. Kirkpatrick, Joey, ill. II. Title
PZ7.K63584P1   1994
[E]—dc20   93-13712

First edition
A B C D E

Printed in Singapore

The illustrations in this book were done in casein paint
on Arches watercolor paper.
The display type was set in Kennerly italic and Ovidius by Harcourt Brace
Photocomposition Center, San Diego, California.
The text type was set in Goudy Oldstyle by Central Graphics,
San Diego, California.
Color separations by Bright Arts, Ltd., Singapore
Printed and bound by Tien Wah Press, Singapore
Production supervision by Warren Wallerstein and Kent MacElwee
Designed by Lydia D'moch

We are grateful to Debra Frasier, Margaret Todd Maitland,
Virginia Jenni Kirkpatrick, Bart Schneider, Diane Natrop for
devoted child care, Kathy and Anne Sawyer, and the staff of
the Iowa Living History Farms.

Special thanks to Flora Carrie Mace for helping us find Plowie
again.

—P. K. and J. K.

In memory of
Florence Cage Kirkpatrick Worden
(1899–1985)

and for
Kristine Kirkpatrick and Tracy Kirkpatrick
Simone and Anton Schneider
Kyra, Adam, and Jacob Levine

A long time ago when there were still horses on the road,
a little girl lived with her mother and father and sister
in a wooden house in Iowa.

All around her was the prairie, and in its thick grass
red-winged blackbirds and meadowlarks
scattered their songs.

Each day when her chores were done,
the girl walked through switchgrass and clover
to see what was there.
Pink thistle and goldfinches, a family of quail,
milkweed, and cream wild indigo.

The earth of the prairie was rich and black,
and where her father cleared its good land
he made fields for corn.

At the edge of the wooden house, her grandfather
had planted apple trees.
When the days grew cool, the girl and her sister
sat in the dooryard hitting apples together
until the pulp was juicy and loose inside the skin.
That was the way they liked to eat them.

Winter was long and brought darkness
and cold to the wooden house.
The work of the family went on.
The girl's mother kneaded dough for loaves of bread.
Her sister turned twelve and, as was the custom,
took charge of the family washing,
leaving less time to play and mush apples.

Snow fell, then drifted.
Her father made his way to the barn every day
to feed the horses and cow
and repair plow points and harnesses
that hung along the wall.
When it wasn't too cold, the girl went with him
to shell corn for the rooster and chickens.

What good was a hurry in winter?
When they couldn't get to school,
the girl stood at the window
and stared at the deepening snow.

Nobody knew where she was, she thought,
and nobody would ever come to visit.
How she wanted to walk in the grass again!

At last water began to drip from the roof.
Slowly spring opened the smell of the earth.
Snow slumped into puddles around the house,
and the first robins flew back.

It was time to get the horse team out, plow the earth,
and plant spring seed again.

So the girl followed her father through the field,
which turned in furrows from the plow.

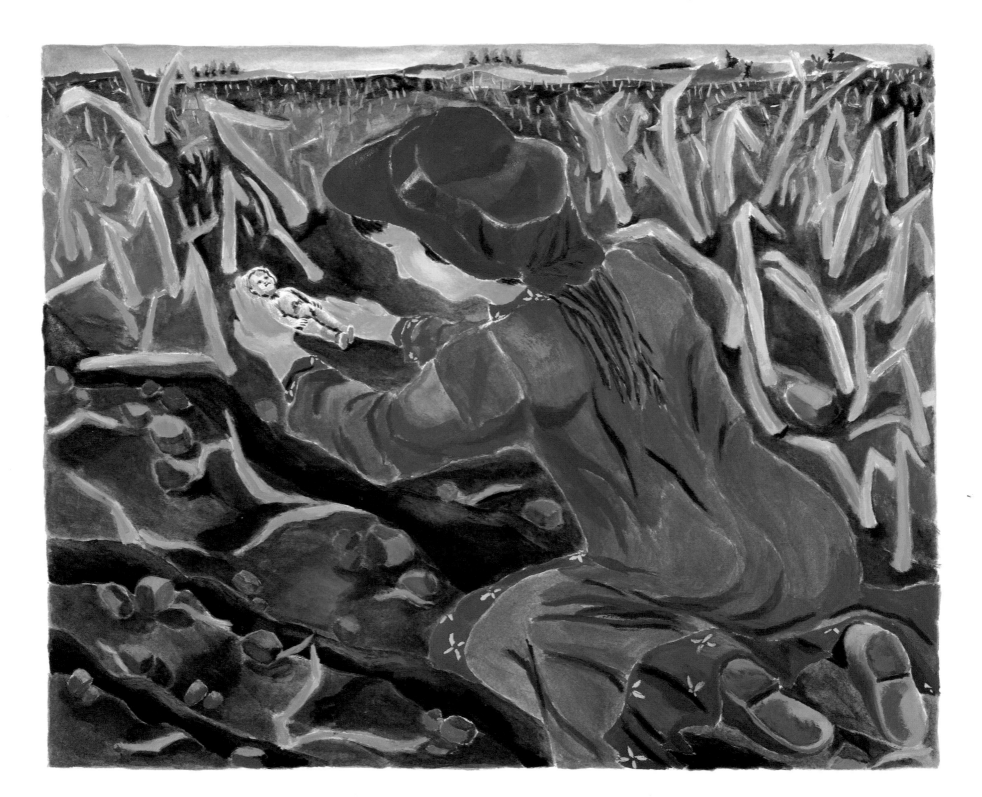

One day the plow point knocked against something
that sprang from the earth like a grasshopper,
and the girl ran to see it.

But instead of a grasshopper she found a doll,
a porcelain figure that fit in her palm.
The doll had a still face like a coin's
and held her arms at her sides.
The soil of the prairie
lay in all the grooves of her body.

Where had the doll come from?
Who lost her?
How long had she been in the earth?

The girl's mother said the doll must have fallen
from a wagon train going over their land fifty years before.
No, her father said, it fell out of somebody's pocket
last summer at the Sunday school picnic.
Her sister looked up from the garden and smiled.
She was tending turnips and hollyhocks
and left the girl alone with her questions.

The girl called the doll Plowie.
Now when she walked on the prairie
she put Plowie in her pocket.
Together they found feathers and wild roses,
and stopped to rest
under branches of an apple tree.

At home the girl kept Plowie in a tobacco tin
stuffed with red gingham.
Wondering where Plowie came from
always made the girl wonder
how she got to be where she was.
As much as she loved the prairie,
she hoped someday to see someplace else.

That summer she washed Plowie in the rain barrel.
In fall she got Plowie sticky with apple juice.
In winter they waited for spring.
And so the years passed.

The girl lived in the wooden house
until she grew up, moved to a city nearby,
married, and had three sons.

Every summer she and her family took the train
to visit her sister in California.
She saw mountains, the ocean, and cities on hills.
When she came home, there was Plowie,
next to the teacup her grandmother's mother
brought from Ireland.

The girl's sons grew up and had children of their own,
who visited her, their grandmother.
As a young girl she had found Plowie.

"Well, look who's here!" the grandmother cried
each time the grandchildren came.
The grandchildren rushed to the what-not,
where they begged to hold Plowie
and to hear the story of the doll who came from the earth.
So the grandmother, who had once lived on the prairie,
took down the doll from her shelf and told them
how she went with her father to follow the plow
and found Plowie.

Where had the doll come from?
Who lost her?
How long had she been in the earth?

One granddaughter especially loved Plowie,
so her grandmother gave her the doll.
The granddaughter took Plowie home
and sewed her a dress of pink calico.

When the granddaughter grew up,
she put Plowie in a china hutch
for her children to see.
And those children wanted to know
where Plowie had come from,
who lost the doll,
and how Great-grandmother had found her.

Now almost a hundred years have passed
since the girl found Plowie.
Plowie is still in the china hutch
where everyone can see her,
but the prairie and the wooden house and the apple trees
are gone.

No one will ever know the name of the child
who lost the porcelain doll on the prairie so many years ago.
But you can still hear the songs of blackbirds and meadowlarks
if you visit that part of the country.
And everyone who hears Plowie's story
gets to keep her forever.

A Note from the Author and Illustrator

Plowie is the name our grandmother gave to a porcelain doll she found while following her father's plow in the first years of this century. Her family's Polk County farm was located in the northwest corner of what is now Des Moines. Iowa became a state in 1846, and by 1860, most of the actual tallgrass prairie had been cultivated. In 1900 Polk County farms typically were 160 acres, with about half the land cultivated in oats, hay, and corn. Spring and fall plowing were done with oxen or a team of two horses, often Percherons. The point of the hand-held plow dug about six inches deep and left a slice of earth at its side.

The doll our grandmother found probably was made in Germany in the late nineteenth century. Such dolls still turn up in Iowa gardens, as well as in antique stores around the country. With our sisters, we often heard Grandma Kirk speak of Plowie, and we all revered the little doll that sat on Grandma's what-not. Our sister Kris keeps Plowie today in Grandma's old china hutch.

Before we were born, the field where Plowie was found had been turned into a parking lot. Yet whenever we passed that place as children we felt a sense of mystery and possibility because Grandma had found Plowie there. Our grandmother had a crackling laugh, she told a good story, and she loved history, especially the commemorations of family life and their connection to the larger story of community and nation. For us, Plowie has come to represent the stories and gifts that lie buried in many fields, in many families, waiting for the plow that will force them up and the loving hands that will catch and care for them.

—Patricia Kirkpatrick and Joey Kirkpatrick